Thomas Bloomer Balch

Reminiscences of Georgetown, D.C.

A Lecture Delivered in the Methodist Protestant Church, Georgetown, D.C., January 20, 1859

Anatiposi

Thomas Bloomer Balch

Reminiscences of Georgetown, D.C.

A Lecture Delivered in the Methodist Protestant Church, Georgetown, D.C., January 20, 1859

Reprint of the original, first published in 1859.

1st Edition 2023 | ISBN: 978-3-38232-720-0

Anatiposi Verlag is an imprint of Outlook Verlagsgesellschaft mbH.

Verlag (Publisher): Outlook Verlag GmbH, Zeilweg 44, 60439 Frankfurt, Deutschland
Vertretungsberechtigt (Authorized to represent): E. Roepke, Zeilweg 44, 60439 Frankfurt, Deutschland
Druck (Print): Books on Demand GmbH, In de Tarpen 42, 22848 Norderstedt, Deutschland

Reminiscences of Georgetown, D.C.

A LECTURE

DELIVERED IN THE METHODIST PROTESTANT CHURCH,
GEORGETOWN, D. C., JANUARY 20, 1859,

BY

REV. T. B. BALCH.

———◆◆◆———

WASHINGTON:
HENRY POLKINHORN, PRINTER.
1859.

TO

DR. BENJAMIN BOHRER,

THE OLDEST SURVIVING PUPIL

OF THE GEORGETOWN CLASSICAL SCHOOL,

LONG SINCE UNDER THE CARE OF THE REVEREND DAVID WILEY,

THIS LECTURE

IS RESPECTFULLY DEDICATED, BY

THE AUTHOR.

REMINISCENCES, &c.

It is common in the Old World to write out the history of towns and cities. Even the obscurest hamlet is not overlooked in the fond attachment of its inhabitants. Thus the Annals of Selborne, in England, have been recorded, together with its Botany and Ornithology. The plants which grow on its environs, and the birds which frequent its trees, have not escaped the observation of its historian. The same is true of Boldre, in the shire of Hants: Its free schools have been noticed, and its forest scenery has been sketched by the pencil of the Rev. William Gilpin, who for many years was the vicar of its lowly church. Numerous instances of Town History might be given, but it is deemed to be unnecessary before the audience now assembled.

The Americans up to the present date have not been so attentive to their localities as the people of England, and other countries which might be mentioned;—indeed in many places our citizens have been proverbial for a lukewarmness amounting to a kind of total indifference. This unconcern probably springs from the fact that town annals seldom rise to an historical dignity. Towns do not wage war; they possess but a small part of the commerce of a country; they are designed for social and municipal life, on a comparatively contracted scale; and they require the lapse of time to give them interest. Therefore, many of our fellow-townsmen may read Motley's "History of the Dutch Republic," Prescott's "Philip the Second," Carlyle's "Frederic the Great," or even that nondescript work called "Abbott's Life of Napoleon," who have never asked after the origin of a place in which they and their posterity have been introduced to the sweets of existence. But interest on this subject will certainly increase as the wheel of Time shall disperse more of its moss over these dwellings. We live here among the mists of more than a hundred years, and it is time for us to be listening to our brief, simple, but impressive story. For this purpose, one appears before you to-night whom you have long known. You will hear him not as a stranger but as a native, and as one who spent his youthful days among these hills, before their greenness had been stripped off by the march of improvement. My audience will not—they cannot—hear as critics one who has been far away to places of education; who has traversed the lowlands of Maryland, the prairies of the West, and the mountains of Virginia; but who, on every new sight of this place, has never failed to exclaim, in the rapture of his feelings—

"This is my own romantic town!"

My first duty in this lecture is to say a word about the origin of Georgetown. How came we to exist as a social Corporation? In answer to this question, we remark, that our town traces its beginning back to the nineteenth day of September, seventeen hundred and fifty-one. On that day the act of the Maryland Assembly took effect which authorized the planting of a new town on the Potomac, and the vending of the lots; some of which (lying where the Market-House now stands) belonged to Colonel George Beall, and others to George Gordon. It appears from documents which are accessible that the Assembly (by commissioners) fixed the rates at which each lot was to be sold. This unparalleled assumption of power on the part of the Assembly of Maryland drew from Colonel Beall a spirited protest, with the threat of an appeal to George the Second, then the sovereign of England. He regarded his title to the lots as beyond all question;—and surely purchasers are not to judge for proprietors of the value of commodities which they owned. This would be to defeat all the laws of trade, and all the ends of justice. His title was probably obtained in the following way: He was son of Ninian Beall, who emigrated to the Patuxent river in Maryland from the shire of Dumbarton, Ayr, or Fife, in Scotland. Ninian Beall might have purchased such title as Patuxent Indians could sell, to certain allotments of land on the west of Rock creek. By inheritance they fell into the possession of his son George; and to defend his property he had set up his tent in the woods, but a few hundred yards from this edifice, on the grounds occupied by the Seminary of Miss English. He was a man of martial air, and some military talents, especially in Indian warfare; for there is a vote of thanks to him on record by the Assembly of Maryland, passed 1699, in which they give him seventy-five pounds sterling, for his bravery in driving back the Indians of the Susquehannah, and causing the surrender of forts held by the adherents of James the Second. The lecturer has read the resolutions by which that expression of confidence in his courage and enterprise was accompanied. There was no estoppel, however, to the sale, and Colonel Beall was so far appeased that he never prosecuted his appeal to the justice of the Mother Country. The lecturer regrets that he has not been able to discover the exact year in which Ninian Beall left Scotland; but it certainly was before the accession of William, Prince of Nassau, to the throne of England, in right of Mary his wife, probably 1669. But from some circumstances connected with his memory, we are induced to think that Dumbarton was the part of Scotland from which he came to Maryland. If so, he could not have come from any one of its shires more abundant in noble objects, or replete with more exquisite scenery. This intrepid emigrant had gazed often on the Rock and Castle of Dumbarton, or reposed in the shadow of Ben Lomond, or strayed along the margin of its unrivalled Lake and the pastoral banks of the Levin, so celebrated by the muse of Smollett. Possibly he had seen the most of those secluded burns which send down the tribute of their waters to the noble Clyde.

But suppose we return a moment to that day in September on which our town was born, in sight of the Potomac. It then breathed, though the infant was for a long time cradled in the woods, and anointed by the fragrance of the *noxious weed*. About its subsequent growth there is no mistake, but the day alluded to is worthy of our remembrance. As it was near the time of the equinoctial storm, we may imagine that the rude and plain sires of the hamlet convened about the lots to be disposed of in showers of rain. We can imagine them as well saturated by the moisture falling from the clouds, with their overcoats buckled round their waists, and holding on to their umbrellas at every dash of the wind. We can imagine the displeasure of Colonel Beall, which, however, was quelled far more quickly than was the wrath of Achilles at the siege of Troy. But we would much rather suppose that the nineteenth of September, 1751, was one of those mild days which Autumn so frequently bestows on our town, when the human affections revel abroad among objects illuminated everywhere by the sun. Perhaps it was a day which stood as a frontispiece to an Indian Summer. Perhaps the Potomac was shining in radiance, and the birds were singing on the boughs of the forest. And when the lots were sold, our forefathers no doubt returned to such tenements as they owned, to speculate on the ire of Colonel Beall, on the consequences of an appeal to King George, and the future destinies of that imaginary Rome they had founded. And in the sequel of events it was in some respects a real Rome, the foundations of which had been laid. Nor was there any Remus to leap over the wall, in the way of contempt.

Colonel Ninian Beall died at the age of one hundred and seven, and was buried probably at Fife Largs, one of his farms on the Eastern Branch, in sight of Washington. His son George died in this place, aged seventy-eight, and was buried in the family ground where Robert Dick now resides. The Bealls intermarried with the Brookes and Magruders—the former of whom came to Maryland in 1650, and the latter in 1655. The Magruders were the *McGregors*, whose lands skirted the eastern side of Loch Lomond.

Having thus marked the origin of our town, it may be well to spend a few minutes in analyzing the sources from which our population has been drawn. The annals of a corporation do not consist so much in the leveling of hills, in the elevation of ravines, in the graduation of streets, or the introduction of gas, as in the social qualities, and the moral, intellectual, and religious habits of the people. The former things may add to the material comfort of the inhabitants, but they are of small account, provided they leave the citizens rude, fierce, or immersed in ignorance. Our population has indeed become a municipal unit, but the unit has been drawn from fractions which successively arrived from different points of the compass. / The town, then, has been supplied with its inhabitants from several counties in Maryland, from Philadelphia, from New England, from Holland, from Old England, from Scotland, from Ireland, and some few from France, who escaped the volcanoes of Gallic Revolution, and who had witnessed the march of the people from Versailles to Paris, headed by Louis the Sixteenth, whose crown at that time was as tremulous as the leaves of the aspen. The Marylanders brought with them those warm, generous feelings, and that easy, refined hospitality, for which they have been so long distinguished. Before leaving their native spots, they had been accustomed to amusements common at that time in the lower counties of Maryland, and which had been derived from the gentry of England. Among these were the chase and the art of angling—the first of which has been represented by Somerville, of Warwick, in England; and the last by the renowned Isaac Walton, who spread his net on every hedge along the River Lea. To persons of such tastes, what could have been more inviting than our broad Potomac, the waves of which are constantly changing from green to blue, and blue to green? It may be advantageously compared with any other stream, from its sources in the Alleghanies to where it empties into Chesapeake Bay. It once entered into a kind of conspiracy with the Shenandoah to rend a passage through the Blue Ridge, and in its course created falls superior to any on the Rhine or the Clyde. But all lovers of the picturesque, and even artists by profession, have acknowledged that its sterner features are exchanged before our town for those of comparative softness. The Potomac has been the fountain of untold happiness to our people, whether they had removed to this place from a distance, or whether indigenous to our chartered limits. We still rejoice in its noble waves; in its triangular rocks; its romantic hills, covered with the red blossoms of the peach, or the snowy blossoms of the apple; in Analostan, and its beaches; in its coves; its mulls; its boats; its aqueducts, and the canals which it feeds. As this paper will consist more of sketches than of history, allow me to assure this audience, that in my boyish days, we have seen anglers whose skiffs have darted to every cape of the river. My eye has seen them starting out in the gray of the morning, or returning home in the twilight of the evening, under stains which the sun had introduced among western clouds, their baskets laden with golden perch. And beneath the radiance of the moon we have heard bands of music on its waters, and horns of uncommon richness and power sounding from boats arriving at our wharves. This was the Arcadian period of our settlement, but we have now become more practical and less social in our habits. Hospitality is below par, and business has become the order of the day, and even of the night; and then we have gained nothing by the change. We must try to raise the former heat of sociability from zero to at least a well-tempered fervor, or else snow will bury the settlement, and icicles may be suspended on all our dwellings. Because we cannot keep pace with the expensive fashions of Washington, there is no reason that the antique, plain, and unvarnished hospitality of our fathers and mothers, our brothers and sisters, our uncles and aunts, should not be immediately revived. But far be it from me to reflect on a people who are objects of love to the lecturer, and not of vituperation. These remarks are intended as kind to all; for a return to our old ways will be promotive both of contentment and cheerfulness. Let us resolve to be social rather than fashionable, and generous instead of extravagant. But a part of our population was drawn from Philadelphia. When the Seat of Government was removed from that city to Washington, at the beginning of the present century, many who had been officially connected with the Government appeared in these parts, to which they had heretofore been strangers. At that time, Georgetown was *the City;* it was more advanced in all the comforts of living, and so continued for many subsequent years. We were a town of at least some consideration when they were felling trees and grading streets and opening avenues in what is now Washington. This place received members of Congress at that time, foreign ambassadors, clerks in the several Departments, and even officers of the Cabinet. In this way some of our most valuable citizens were obtained. Individuals might be mentioned, without any violation of propriety, but it is my intention rather to classify the inhabitants than to individualize. If emigrants be *men*, we care but little from what quarter of the world they may come. We measure them here by their virtues, and not by parallels of latitude or meridian lines or titles of nobility. It is indifferent to us whether they come from the banks of the Delaware or out of Siberia; from Peruvian valleys or the Ural mountains. Let them come, if they wear about them the attributes of a common humanity. They may come, if they please, even in swarms, provided they add to the hum of industry or to the sweetness of social and civic life. But New England has supplied no unimportant part of our population, from time to time. We are indebted principally to the town of Newburyport, in Massachusetts, situated on the Merrimack river, for some of our most useful and industrious citizens. We avoid names, simply because they are too numerous to be mentioned. Such are the links of connection between Newburyport and Georgetown, that the lecturer once made a visit to the Massachusetts settlement, and for three weeks he received at that place nothing but one stream of flowing hospitality. It was a hospitality rather more formal than ours; but still it was sincere, genuine, and princely. The town was left with the deepest regret, after officiating in several of its churches, and among them was the church on Federal street, in which the ashes of Whitfield (that astonishing evangelist) are buried. Since that time a monument has been built over his remains by William Bartlett, a man of abundant wealth, and of large munificence. We have named Holland as a country from which a portion of our people have come; nor could they have come from a province more beloved at home or respected abroad. It was the last of the seventeen provinces in its resistance to the measures of Margaret of Parma, and the first to renew the contest against the Inquisition of Philip the Second, under the lead of William the Silent. The Dutch are a neat, industrious, and great people. Their ships have rolled among the waves of the most distant seas; they have collected plants from all the latitudes; they have culled flowers from the central waist of the world; they have explored torrid and frozen zones; they have swept the Thames in defiance of Blake, the great British Admiral; they have revolutionized England by the diplomacy of the Prince of Orange; they have saved the Protestant religion; they have planted flourishing colonies among the spice islands of the Orient; they have bestowed on the world scholars like Grotius of Delft Haven, and Erasmus of Rotterdam, and such martyrs to Liberty as Egmont and Hoorne, and such Admirals as Vantromp and De Ruyter. The historians, dramatists, and artists, of Holland have been numerous; nor as Americans ought we ever to forget, that out of Delft Haven the group of men, women, and children went forth into the broad and wintry seas, who arrived at Plymouth Rock in the December of 1620. Is there a man, then, in this assembly who regrets that Holland helped to populate this our beloved town? Not one, we will venture to affirm. And permit me here to say that many have resided in this town who first saw the light of this world in Ireland. Many such are buried in our graveyards. They preferred our hills and woods to the emerald fields and the shamrock nooks of Erin, because America was free and Ireland was enslaved. And yet Ireland has produced great men to plead her cause. The voice of Grattan was lifted up against the annihilation of the Irish Parliament, and that of Robert Emmet, in the immediate prospect of an ignominious death. The eloquent tongue of Curran was employed in defence of her martyrs. The bugle of Wellington thrilled the heart of Napoleon at Waterloo—and Wellington was an Irishman. With inimitable pathos has Goldsmith sketched the ruin of its villages, and Swift vindicated the currency of his country. But in these unpretending reminiscences it would be going far astray to commit myself to the complicated affairs of Ireland—her immense troubles, the furnace of persecution through which she has passed, her rights trampled down by her English oppressors, and the long catalogue of her distinguished men. The sandal-tree is said to anoint with fragrance the axe by which it is leveled to the dust; and Ireland has dispersed over England the tints of taste and of letters. Now it gives me pleasure to state that an emigrant from this greenest isle of the sea was once elevated to the Mayoralty of this town by our unbought suffrages. He was from the county of Clare, in the west of Ireland, and he came to this place without friends or patrons, but he depended on the probity of his character and the amenity of his feelings. His kindness to boys is a recollection cherished by the lecturer to this day; and it is my sincere wish that Thomas Corcoran (once the Mayor of Georgetown) may not easily be forgotten. To one of his descendants* we are indebted for Oakwood Cemetery, to which so much of the talent and beauty of our town have already been committed. That sacred acre begins at the apex of Dumbarton Hill, and slopes downward to Rock Creek, on shelves crowded with memorial flowers that wear those pensive hues that become the spot that divides between those who still live and those who have lived. The Swiss chapel on the hill, the murmuring of the waters below, the half-shade and half-

---

* W. W. Corcoran.

sunlight of the ground, the snow-like mounds, the sepulchral records, the marble lettered by the hand of Friendship, the clumps of wood and beds of violets,—will long be in unison with our feelings as we tread those gravelled walks, that we may read the touching elegy not written in a book but on hallowed soil. There reposes the dust of many whom we valued and loved throughout their earthly career. There slumbers the gallant Towson, whose heart never quailed before his country's foes; and Morris, who stopped the Guerriere on her march over the mountain wave. All honor, say I, to the individual who planned and to him who executed that work of sepulchral taste, which might well fix for a while the gaze of Death himself, ere he spur on his pale steed to that goal at which he has won myriads of pensive wreaths !

In tracing the connections of this town with foreign parts, we must ask the indulgence of this audience whilst we introduce for a few minutes a group of seven Scotch families who arrived among us in 1785. This event took place eight or nine years before the lecturer was born, but it subsequently left an impression on his memory, never to be effaced. They were from the town of Forres, which stands on the Findhorn, in the northeastern shire of Maury. They had relinquished many fond endearments at home, in seeking their fortunes in a distant land. They had left the noble Loch Spinie, with its swans; the bridge of the Findhorn; the moor of Forres, immortalized by the genius of Shakspeare; the dilapidated cathedral of Elgin; the trout and salmon of contiguous streams; the traditions connected with the Castle of Inverness; their parish kirk; the stone manse of their pastor,—and many other objects too numerous to be mentioned. After them came the Rev. William Allen, who had been educated at Marischal College, at Aberdeen, the northern capital of Scotland. He was a man of some peculiarities, but they were harmless. He taught for years in our town. Never was a pupil so proud as he of a preceptor. Dr. Beattie, who was a native of Lawrence Kirk, in Kincardinshire, had been Professor of Moral Philosophy in the College which stands in the northeast of Aberdeen, at the time that our emigrant was pursuing his classical course. This incident colored all his colloquies about Dr. Beattie, and with the most amiable fondness he dwelt on the charms of the Minstrel, on his answer to Hume, on his friendship for Lady Montague, and on the pension he received from the Crown of England. It is my belief that all who constituted this original stock of emigration are now deceased, but they have left descendants who may well be proud of their sires. The last survivor requested the lecturer to perform her funeral rites, which was sacredly done in compliance with that request. And never was there a better woman than the last of that Scotch Mohican band, for she was generous even to a fault. She died, too, with astonishing fortitude, and with many tender reminiscences of Forres, requesting that her pall-bearers should all be chosen from the descendants of the Scotch. It would give me pleasure to dwell at length on this part of my subject, because one of my earliest recollections is my marvelling from what part of the world these people had come. My mind was first set on the study of geography by a desire to find out this secret. When the Portuguese discovered the Canary Isles, the people of those Islands wondered that the discoverers should have come down from the clouds. They had supposed that their little strips of earth were the whole world, and to a child Georgetown was the world. But my illusions were soon dissipated by emigrants whose houses were like Robin Hood's men in Sherwood forest, all standing in a row. And such are the undying impressions of childhood that the lecturer never reads a book of Scotch theology, a volume of Scotch history, a dissertation from any Scotch philospher, any translation made by George Buchanan, any poem by a Caledonian bard, any description of a loch, glen, burn, straith, moorland, ben, mull, cairn, or anything else, without recurring to the band from Forres, who threw the peculiar hues of their country over our town. Let, us, then continue, as we have ever done, to revere the land where St. Columba dispersed the light of learning among uncultivated barbarians; where Wallace nobly parted with his life; where Bruce stood a conqueror against English aggression; where Watt improved the steam-engine; where Grahame sung the repose of the Sabbath, and Burns the Ingleside, and Logan the braes of Yarrow, and where Sir Walter Scott collected spoils for romance from the Tweed to the Orkneys, and from Montrose to the Hebrides.

Some persons have requested me to introduce a few anecdotes into these reminiscences, as productive of good feeling. Anecdotes have always been popular. Whole volumes of them have been published from time to time, and incidents somewhat playful have always amused persons who attend lectures. We recollect a circumstance which will serve to show the great progress which astronomical science had made in our town about 1805. A writing-master had come from Prince William, Virginia, who professed to teach that art in twenty lessons. The lecturer was among his pupils. This teacher was a small man; he wore his hat on the side of his head, and he was so self-consequential that, according to his self-conceit, he knew more than Sir Isaac Newton or Kepler. Left alone with him one day after all the other boys had retired, he remarked to me very gravely, " My little gentleman, as you advance on the stage of life you will encounter various attempts to shake your principles. The delusion is getting abroad, even in this town, that the stars are inhabited, but my views on that point differ widely from those of Sir Isaac Newton, though he be the greatest philosopher of the present times. Have you never," continued he, "seen the stars of a summer night shoot away from their orbits? Then what becomes of the people by whom they were inhabited?" He was so animated by his subject that he walked to and fro over the floor for twenty minutes, declaiming against the views which have since become current. To me his logic seemed irresistible, being myself unable at the time to distinguish between a star and a meteor. But though not a great philosopher, our teacher was a great penman, particularly in the German text. And if another writing-master should come among us, permit me to suggest to boys the importance of a good hand. Senator Choate once wrote me a letter, and it has taken me ten years to conjecture its meaning, for the writing was like the impression which a chicken makes when it scratches in the snow. My reply, of course, proceeded on the principle of guessing at his meaning.

There are some here to-night who remember Pechion, that bland and elegant Frenchman who was sent out by Bonaparte, in 1803, to receive the sixteen millions which we paid for Louisiana. He was a Huguenot from Lyons, on the Rhone, where he now resides. He must be more than ninety years of age, and we will venture to say that when the patriarch walks up or down the streets of that city, the boys and girls suspend golden violets on his staff. When here he was exceedingly popular with us boys, for he would stop to look upon our games of marbles, upon our juvenile musters, and he would himself set up pieces of coin in the crevices of the posts to be shot out by Chickasaw and Choctaw Indians. One fourth of July the lecturer, having then reached the patriarchal age of eight years, was to deliver a grandiloquent oration to his comrades, in Scotch row. But lo! at the time appointed there was no audience. Captain Doughty's company was on parade in the old orchard, and drums were beating and fifes were sounding at the square of the town, and yet that oration was too important to be lost. In fact, it seemed to the little orator that he must die before sundown unless some besides his comrades should hear that wonderful piece of eloquence, and Jefferson and Adams had not then set the example of dying on that day. At that time Pechion and General Mason lived close to each other, near the Bank of Columbia, and you must all see that it was a point gained to get as my hearers a Minister Plenipotentiary and the General of all our militia. Accordingly, the orator of the day hopped, skipped, and jumped after them, and they both came. Now, some persons have asked after the cause of my undying hostility to Napoleon. My reply is, on that fourth of July a resolution was made, if Bonaparte ever maltreated my friend Pechion, he should find in me a decided foe, and on his return to Paris the Emperor behaved rudely to the Georgetown Ambassador. If Hannibal was true to the vow he took, at eight years old, of hostility to Rome, the Georgetown lad will not falter in fidelity to *his* so long as life may last.

You have all heard of John Randolph, of Roanoke, who spent so many Congressional terms in our town. His infirmities, however, increased with advancing years. One midnight he took a notion that he would die before morning; but there was "one thing," said the orator to his servant, "that can save my life." "What is it?" answered Juba, who had long been used to the caprices of his master. "Don't you know?" he replied. "What, what but a glass of Georgetown water?" His servant took the hint and started, but not liking to be taken into custody, he took a glass out of a well on Capitol hill, after lingering long enough to inspire a belief that he had come over to town. When he handed it to his master the eyes of the orator glistened again, and he said to his servant, "Juba, did you ever hear of the nectar of Chios? This is like what the heathen deities used to drink in old times. The country is falling fast into despotism, and to-morrow my voice shall ring and squeak in the Capitol against the Sultans."

Let us now return a moment to the foundation of our town. We suppose that it slumbered on in that drowsiness which is common to all hamlets. Probably it was somewhat startled from its propriety by the defeat of General Braddock, which took place in 1755. We may well imagine the consternation of its inhabitants, more especially as Braddock marched for Turtle creek, near Pittsburgh, where he fell, from Alexandria. But tranquility succeeds to the most alarming events, and it is possible that the people went quietly on in the cultivation of tobacco, and in rearing the warehouses in which that juicy commodity was stowed away. In my boyhood, one of those warehouses was standing directly opposite Scotch row. This ear of mine has often heard from its interior roof the twittering of a thousand swallows, as they were triumphantly building their nests out of the slime of the Potomac. The article, or the weed injurious, was exported to Amsterdam, Bremen, and Hamburgh. So long as our channel was unobstructed, noble ships used to bind themselves to our wharves, and many a gay streamer has floated between Analostan Island and our town. The people were exceedingly jealous of their maritime rights; and when the long bridge was reared across the Potomac, about 1807, our whole population was thrown into a muss. Public meetings were called, speeches were made, and protests circulated. The schoolboys were quite transported at this excitement, for our teacher, the Rev. David Wiley, had entered so deeply into the controversy, that he would either dismiss us of his own accord, or throw out an unmistakable hint that we might ask him for a holiday; and then he would hie to the Capitol and listen to the speeches in Congress. Bridges have sometimes been important things. There was one built by Xerxes over the Hellespont, and another by Cæsar, and another still by Napoleon, over the Berisina. Those of Lodi, Jena, and one over the Thames, in honor of Wellington, are quite suggestive. But not one of them was reared in the face of greater opposition than the structure to which allusion has been made. But the Alexandrians carried their point, and then our people fell back on the rather doubtful consolation that the bridge could not survive the assaults of the ice which used to accumulate to enormous masses in our old-fashioned winters; and several times parts of it have been swept away, but it will not totally disappear. It is always renewed by the action of Congress, and that to the injury of our commerce. The arrival of ships at a town is not without its influence in expanding the human mind and affections. No man can look at the quays of Liverpool, or the vessels of the Nore, without dispatching his thoughts to all parts of the world. Nor does any artist deem his picture of a town complete unless he has introduced its shipping on the canvas. The Boat Argo, the Mariners of England, by Campbell, the Ancient Mariner of Coleridge, and the lines of Horace to the ship which was to convey Virgil to Athens, show what a spell sea objects throw over the imagination. You all remember that splendid ship, the General Lingan. She was lost between Savannah and Baltimore, in consequence of her being overladen with lumber, but not until her prow had touched many distant strands, and scaled many mountain billows. Her commander, Captain Fairbank, with eight other men, clung on to her keel for nine weary days and nights, and he and two others were taken from the wreck in an unconscious state and conveyed safely to Baltimore. General Lingan, after whom the ship was named, had fallen a victim to political violence during the war of 1812, and he was buried in this place with military honors, and his funeral eulogy was pronounced by Parke Custis, of Arlington. In my humble judgment, this was by far the best intellectual effort ever made by the old chronicler. It was brief, comprehensive, forcible, and pathetic. But during all the interval from 1751 to 1783, when peace was made between Great Britain and the United States, we can easily realize the condition of our town. George

Third stood in need, as he supposed, of a new palace. This led him to place an unknown tax on the colonies, and Dr. Johnson wrote his celebrated pamphlet entitled "Taxation no Tyranny." My father has repeatedly told me that the ladies of Georgetown positively refused to drink tea during the progress of the Revolution. Even the cups used at his wedding, in the year 1782, and which are now in the possession of the heirs of Major Jewell, were not much larger than a thimble. This course was quite patriotic on the part of our ladies, provided it were not the black tea, for black tea is nothing better than so much wormwood and gall. If it were the green beverage which they abnegated, then were the ladies of Georgetown worthy to be enrolled with the mother and sisters of Coriolanus, who saved Rome at her most eventful hour.

Reminiscences of various kinds are now crowding upon me which evince the strength of the social affections. They consist of parties of innocent amusement; of water excursions; of boat races which came off on the Potomac; of military musters; of companies made up to visit the Great Falls or Analostan Island; of the old orchard which stood not more than a bowshot from the church now occupied by Dr. Norwood; of bees that rode from sunrise to nightfall on their flowery chariots; of young officers who enlivened the Union Hotel after the Tripolitan war, in 1804; of beautiful young ladies, who married and then went to a distance; of distinguished men who resided here for a time, or paid us a transient visit, such as Count Volney, Baron Humboldt, Fulton, Talleyrand, Jerome Bonaparte, Pechion, General St. Clair, Washington Irving, the Roanoke orator, Luther Martin, and Barent Gardenier, the last of whom was unfortunately shot in a duel, in 1807, by George Washington Campbell, of Nashville, Tennessee. Or we might indulge in recollections of such grotesque characters as old Yarrah, who was a Mohammedan from Guinea, and of whom an admirable likeness was taken by Simpson, or of Lorenzo Dow, the great itinerant, whose weary limbs found their final repose in one of our graveyards. Or we might call to mind the few literary tints which have been dispersed over our town. Pascal's Provincial Letters, Malthus on Population, Mrs. Opie's Tales, Dr. Watts on the Improvement of the Mind, and other works, have been issued from our press. The author of the Star-spangled Banner, Francis S. Key, was one of our distinguished barristers. A System of Chemistry was many years ago published here by Dr. Thomas Ewell. A gentleman has recently produced a valuable Commentary on the Apocalypse. The author of the British Spy resided among us for a short time. A female novelist is at present one of our inhabitants. Portions of a profound metaphysical work were written by the Rev. Asa Shinn, in the parsonage of the Methodist Episcopal church. And one of our present citizens, a native of Michigan, has recorded in two volumes his adventures among the wilds of America, after having crept into many tangled bournes, and thrown his net over our northwestern lakes, and angled in many rivers abounding more in trout than the Tay, the Dee, or the Forth. But in recalling such antique things you might take me for an octogenarian, whereas many vernal breezes have yet to fan my locks before you will catch me in the company of such venerable patriarchs. This sketch, however, would be incomplete without some condensed notice of our banks, schools, and churches. Limited to the space of one hour, our remarks of course will be as brief as possible.

The old Bank of Columbia probably went into operation under a charter from Maryland, but it was subsequently re-chartered by Congress. The directors removed the banking house from the business part of the town to an elevation that overlooked the Potomac and Analostan island. Some time since, a friend presented me with a painting of that part of the town which lies between that old Bank and Analostan; and it is that article, in my lowly Virginia cottage, which most frequently prompts my ruminations. If my memory serve me aright, the Union Bank was opened about 1809, and the Farmers' and Mechanics' in 1814, the latter of which is still in existence. Its stock deserves to be at par, for the institution has pursued a wise and liberal course of discounting, in the darkest periods of financial embarrassment. No panic has shaken the confidence of the directors in the integrity of our citizens. The Central Bank had but a short-lived existence; but the Bank of Commerce is still in operation. Passing from these institutions to schools, we remark that some of our schools have been for boys, and some for girls, and some for young ladies, and some for the simple elements of education, and others for classical science. There are few persons so lost to the associations of memory, as not to recall their juvenile pranks. The satchel, the horn-book, the copybook, the primer, the slate, and the birch, are not easily forgotten. They make indelible impressions. They clung fast to Shenstone when he wrote the School Mistress at the Lensowes in Salop, and to Oliver Goldsmith, in his Deserted Village. But the lecturer must not commit himself to the tide of such reminiscences, lest he might be borne out to a sea in which his skiff might be stranded among the Fortunate Islands. Suffice it to say, that hundreds of young ladies have been educated here, from all parts of the country, who are now performing the duties of wives and mothers from the St. Croix to the St. Mary's; and they look back to this town from the magnolias of Florida, from southern savannas, from the Indian mounds of Mississippi, and from the Blue and White Mountains of Virginia and New Hampshire, and, in one instance, at least, from Peterhoff, in Russia. The Catholic College was founded in 1792, principally by the influence of Archbishop Carroll, of Baltimore, and it has educated young men from Maryland, Chili, and the West Indies. Among them was Robert Walsh, author of the celebrated letter on the Genius of the French Government, and the Paris correspondent of the National Intelligencer. The position of the college, as you all know, commands a splendid view of the Potomac, the aqueduct, and the wild, sylvan shores of Virginia. Scarcely had the Lancasterian system of education been made known in England, before it was introduced into this town by a gentleman who had been intimate with its founder, and who died in 1840, deeply regretted as one of our public benefactors. Joseph Lancaster was here in 1821. He was a Quaker; and we ought not to forget that Generals Greene and Brown, West the artist, Clarkson the philanthropist, Gurney the banker, Wiffen the translator of Tasso, Tupper the author of Proverbial Philosophy, Barclay a writer on theology, Bernaed Barton a poet, and Howit a miscellaneous writer, were reared in the same denomination. But the academy with which my largest recollections are connected was the one which stood exactly where the house stands occupied at present by Mrs. Shaafe. The academy was taught by the Rev. David Wiley, who came to this town about 1802, from Northumberland, on the Susquehannah—the town in which Dr. Priestley, a distinguished chemist, died in 1804. Our teacher had graduated with distinction at Nassau Hall; and he was a better mathematician than classic. He taught navigation to Commodore Jesse D. Elliott, who took a part in the action of Lake Erie, in 1813. He was not without some peculiarities of character; but he was a good man, and certainly cultivated a high public spirit, being mayor, librarian, merchant, teacher, and preacher, and keeper of the post-office, at the same time. He finally died in North Carolina, when on a survey, in the employment of the Government. In my boyhood, that locality was a round green hill, where the bees were busy all summer in worrying innumerable flowers. The fate of the pupils has been various. Some perished at sea, some in duels, some from natural causes, and some few survive; and, among the survivors, it gives me pleasure to recall the names of Bohrer, Marbury, and Polkinhorn. If we do not not dwell in recollection on the academies of Dr. Carnahan, McVean, Abbott, Tyng, and others, it is because they were comparatively modern; and we leave this part of the subject, not without

tender recollections of our Susquehannah preceptor—a river sung by a
poet of the Clyde :

> "On Susquehannah's side, fair Wyoming,
>   Although the wild flower on thy ruined wall,
> And roofless homes, a sad remembrance bring
>   Of what thy gentle people did befall,
> Yet thou wert once the loveliest land of all
>   That see the Atlantic wave their morn restore."

The first church founded in this town was German Reformed, and stood
up High street, but a short distance from the Presbyterian grave yard.
It has disappeared, in the lapse of time, and among those changes to
which every town is exposed. The lecturer can recall nothing about it
but the last tinkling given by its simple bell. The Presbyterian church
on Bridge street was erected in 1782, which was two years after its
founder reached this place. Dr. Balch, its founder, was born on Deer
creek, near Baltimore, in 1747, was graduated at Princeton, in 1774, and
died in 1833. Delicacy forbids me from saying more of him than that
he taught a classical academy in this town for many years ; that his an-
cestors were from Wales ; that his brother, the Rev. Hezekiah I. Balch,
of North Carolina, was the first signer of the celebrated Mecklenburg
declaration of independence, in May, 1775, and that he built one of the
earliest brick churches in the settlement. The Catholic church was
erected probably about the same time with the college, in 1790. The
first Methodist Episcopal church was a very small edifice, which was sup-
planted by one more commodious, and at present the congregation wor-
ship in Dumbarton street. The church occupied at present by the first
Episcopal congregation was commenced long before it was finished. The
birds used to build their nests in it, and we boys used to clamber up its
walls. It was completed in 1804, and occupied by the Rev. John Sayrs,
from Port Tobacco, who was a graduate of Princeton College, and a fine
classical scholar. He died in January, 1809 ; and his funeral discourse
was preached by the Rev. William Gibson, of Alexandria, a man of eloquence, but too impulsive for the pulpit. He was succeeded by the Rev.
Walter Addison, one of the meekest and kindest creatures on earth. He
had officiated occasionally in town as far back as 1785. He lived at
Oxen Hill, in sight of Alexandria, and was at one time possessed of a.
princely estate. He had been educated in England ; but he was not descended from Joseph Addison, for the essayist left but one daughter, and
she never married, and he was of Wilts ; but the Addisons of Maryland
came from Cumberland in 1678. The second Episcopal church was finished in 1818, and has been favored with a succession of able pastors.
Among them was Dr. Keith, a fine German scholar. A cloud of insanity

fell on his understanding, but the Star of Bethlehem burned brightly in that cloud. The church in which we are now convened was built in 1829, and it was opened by a discourse from the Rev. Nicholas Sneethen, from the text, " If the Son shall make you free, you will be free indeed." The people of this congregation are now making a praiseworthy effort to pay a debt which they have recently contracted for an edifice they have just built ; and the profits of these lectures are sacredly appropriated to this object.

These reminiscences might certainly be extended into a duodecimo volume ; but, afraid of exhausting your patience, the lecturer must hasten to a close, by a brief statement of our wants as a town. We want a newspaper to represent the place, and it ought to be patronised by all our citizens. We want a lyceum, in which public lectures might be given, connected with a reading-room, where young men might profitably spend their winter evenings. We need a library as good, at least, as the old Columbian Library, which, like the Sibyl leaves, has long since been dispersed. But there was a time when the books of which it was composed yielded great mental enjoyment to the people. Some resorted ever to the shelves, which held the works of Linnæus, and the Asiatic Researches of Sir William Jones. Should we ever be fortunate enough to obtain a library, we ought to exclude the novels of Dickens and Thackeray, because their ambition seems to be to throw human nature into attitudes comic and grotesque. But the novels of Sir Walter Scott might well be admitted, because he swept out of being all the old romances, and gave dignity to this species of composition. He is an admirable writer, whether he depict the age of chivalry in his Ivanhoe, or the love of truth in his Heart of Mid Lothian, or the woes of human affections in his Bride of Lammermoor. We need a literary Review pledged to the union of our States ; and it would be patriotic to start one, could a Jeffrey, Gifford, Lockhart, or Christopher North, be found as its editor. And we need a bridge by which our citizens might pass and repass to and from Washington. Our upper bridge was built by Harbaugh, a Pennsylvanian. Two of these conveniences figure in the poems of Burns, and the new bridge erected at Bristol, England, in the fifteenth century, is quite celebrated in the writings of Chatterton, and the Ivy bridge, in Devonshire, in those of Southey, the former poet laureate. And, through the improvement of Pennsylvania avenue, we shall be favored with an erection worthy of our town at no distant day.

There is one reflection, however, appropriate to the close of this lecture, which ought to be mentioned. Our fathers have passed away, and, by the lapse of time, we are pressing closely on those slopes by which they have descended to their graves. Oakwood, and our other cemeteries, await us all. The one on the heights was begun in 1849, and completed in 1852. It was designed by Captain De la Roche, who was born in New York, in 1791. He still survives, and long may it be before that distinguished engineer shall be borne to its sandstone chapel and through its sylvan gateway. Its poplar, walnut, and chesnut clumps will long stand as his memorial, for he took pains to preserve them whilst shaping even gnarled oaks into proportion. In all that pensive, stereoscopic view which he has embellished, he heard a voice sounding in his ear, like the expostulation of Morris—

"Woodman, woodman, spare that tree."

But, in leaving the stage of action which has been assigned us, so far from wishing to shut out our posterity from the rich heritage we have enjoyed, we bid them welcome. We can cheerfully, at least, if not exultingly, say to our children and children's children, advance and take possession of all that we relinquish. These ranging hills, and quiet docks, and holy kirks, and sunny Sabbaths, have long been ours, but they are handed over to you, not that they may be lost, but enlarged, improved, and embellished for the use of future generations. And so long as we remain, may we ever act under the conviction that except the Lord keep the town, the watchman waketh but in vain. May we place its destinies under the wing of that Creator who never slumbers, and into the noon of whose existence no evening star can ever be introduced. This course is important, for he can send pestilence, if he please, to fill our cemeteries, or the devouring element of fire to lay our dwellings in ashes, or the earthquake to rock all our foundations, as he rocked even Lisbon like a cradle, in 1755, or Caraccas in 1812, or Japan as he has recently done, with all its swarming millions.

Breathes there a man with soul so dead,
Who never to himself has said,
This is my own, my native town.

May we then as a people ever seek Him who maketh the seven stars and Orion, who calleth for the floods of the sea, and poureth them out like water., and who maketh the day dark with clouds. The Lord is his name. "Let Glasgow flourish through the preaching of the Word," is inscribed, even to this day, over the gates of that growing city. No people can long exist without cherishing the institutions of religion. Our safety at the midnight hour is dependent on popular instruction. Above all things, our ambition ought to be to keep sacred the Sabbath day.

Nothing can be more ornamental than the repose of a town one day in each passing week for the private and public duties of Christianity. And may the different denominations of Christians continue to cultivate with each other the spirit of concord. Let us indignantly frown down everything like bigotry and intolerance, and be careful to quench every incipient spark of persecution. Behold how good and pleasant it is for brethren to dwell together in unity. The primitive ministers of this town were catholic in their feelings, and now that they have all escaped beyond the boundaries of time, they experience nothing but emotions of pleasure that, when laboring among us, they lovingly co operated in advancing the cause of law, science, morals, education, and religion.

From the National Intelligencer, November 4, 1853.

It is due to our esteemed neighbors of Georgetown to place in our columns the subjoined interesting retrospect of the worthy men who gave an impulse and steady advance to her prosperity and value to her social circles.

From the Georgetown Independent.

OUR GREAT MEN.—By Jno. T. Bangs.

" Drink waters out of thine own cistern, and running waters out of thine own well."

" The hand of the diligent maketh rich."

The significant, and perhaps to some persons exceptionable title, " Our Great Men," we opine will not startle your readers or disturb the equilibrium of their minds while engaged in the active duties of their respective vocations; while struggling through the entanglements of business pursuits, or while indulging in the gay reveries and day-dreams of this flitting existence. If any effect should be superinduced, may it be to awaken them to a wise consideration of the subject-matter of this communication ; to the forming of a proper estimate of human character as exhibited in every-day life : to a more fixedness of purpose in their pursuits ; to an increased diligence in business ; and may these results become accessories to their profit, exaltation, and usefulness !

We make free, then, to assert that Georgetown can boast of having produced some great men; that is, that it has been either the birth-place, permanent residence, or starting point of many eminent men, who have been or are widely known and appreciated for their great capacities and sterling merit. When we say great men, we do not use the term *great* as applying to literary merit or literary acquirements, but we use it here as especially referring to that distinction which attaches to commercial or mercantile ability and successful enterprise. We hold the opinion that great men can be found or recognised by the attentive observer in all the varied pursuits of life ; men peculiarly adapted by their physical or mental powers to the positions they occupy ; men who draw largely, because entitled thereto, upon the confidence of their fellow-men, and who command the esteem and admiration of the circle in which they move, whether limited or wide-extended.

The biographies of those individuals who will be hereinafter mentioned, who have won for themselves an enviable name—the details of their lives, the means by which they so rapidly accumulated wealth, and became eminent and influential citizens in their day, if sketched by the faithful pen, would furnish striking examples for imitation to many of the present generation of our community, and in all probability exert a controlling influence upon their successors. The untiring industry, remarkable energy, and unimpeachable integrity which were their shining and prominent characteristics, marked by no ordinary success, should offer strong incentives to young merchants to adopt and steadily pursue a similar course in life, alike high-minded, active, and honorable, even if their efforts, unlike their predecessors, were not signalized by the return of rich harvests of wealth and the attainment of wide-spread influence.

Within a few years past some of those prominent citizens have gone down to the silence and repose of the sepulchre. "The pitcher has been broken at the fountain." They rest from their labors, but their light has not gone out. They will always be worthy of honorable mention and remembrance. Memory, ever faithful to her trust, will recall their characters with true picturings to stimulate the living to renewed vigor and perseverance, that they may achieve like fame and even greater. They cannot be recalled too frequently to our notice or consideration. Others are still living, and are enjoying the well-earned confidence and approbation of their fellow-men, steadily progressing, daily adding to their wealth, with liberality almost limitless, and, what is far better and higher, with reputations unsullied. They are beacon-lights to all around them, flashing with benignant brilliancy, radiating far and wide over the pathways of life.

This is a topic we have often had strong inclinations to write upon, and thereafter give to the press, but as often postponed it, deeming ourselves inadequate to the task, however pleasing. We have at this time been urged into the presentation of these and other kindred remarks which we may hereafter make by the following which we have clipped from one of our Northern papers, which you will do me the favor to publish. It is a description of the early difficulties and the after success of G. PEABODY, Esq., the now celebrated London banker, whose liberality has been well tested, and one whose financial ability is unquestioned. Though *now located* upon foreign soil, he has never forgotten the land of his birth. His liberal donations are evidences sufficient to attest this fact. He has gained a high reputation on both sides of the Atlantic. May he long live to enjoy both his fortune and fame! We claim that he commenced his fortunate career in our ancient town, and here gave the first evidences of great business talent.

We have already announced the donation of $30,000 made recently by GEORGE PEABODY, the opulent London Banker, to the town of Danvers, in Massachusetts, the place of his birth, for the establishment of an institution for educational purposes and a library. The corner-stone of the proposed edifice, which is to cost $20,000, was laid on Saturday, the 20th instant. R. S. DANIELS, Chairman of the Board of Trustees, opened the proceedings with a brief speech, in the following portrait of Mr. Peabody:

"The character and history of Mr. Peabody have, by the natural course of things, become so familiar to us within the last year that, like his name, they have almost come to be household property. How, nearly threescore years ago, 'in a very humble house in this then quiet village, he was born, the son of respectable parents, but in humble circumstances;' how, 'from the common schools of the parish, such as they were from

1805 to 1807,' to use his own simple words, he 'obtained the limited education his p a rents' means could afford, but to the principles then inculcated owing much of the foundation for such success as heaven has been pleased to grant him during a long business life;' how, at the early age of eleven years, in the humble capacity of a grocer's boy, in a shop hard by where we now stand, he commenced his life of earnest but successful toil; how, four years after, having sought promotion in another sphere, he found himself, by his father's death and his brother's misfortune, an orphan, without means, without employment, without friends, and all in the most gloomy times: but how, buoyed up by a firm resolve and a high endeavor, he turned his back upon the endeared but now desolate scenes of his boyhood, and sought under a southern sun those smiles of fortune denied him by the frowning skies of his northern home; how there in Georgetown, in the District of Columbia, he became, while not yet nineteen years old— such was his capacity and fidelity—partner in a respectable firm, which afterwards removed to Baltimore, and had branches established in two or three of our principal cities; and how at length he became the head of his house, and, having crossed and re-crossed the ocean many times in the transaction of his foreign business, he at last, in 1847, established himself permanently in London, having now created an immense business and amassed a princely fortune; how, through all this career from poverty to opulence, that simple heart and kindly nature which in youth divided with his orphan brothers and sisters the scanty earnings of his toil, and in later and more prosperous days expanded in social amenities and timely charities to his countrymen in a strange land; how this true nature remained ever the same, untainted by that proud success which too often corrupts, mellowed only by those growing years which seldom fail to blunt our finer sensibilities; and, lastly, how, while with a private life above reproach and a professional character distinguished even among the merchant-princes of England, he had come to be pointed out, both at home and abroad, as the model of a man and a merchant; how, all this time, his 'heart, untravelled, turned fondly' to his country; and how, true to her interests and her honor, in the darkest hour of her adversity he stood up manfully in her defence, and, throwing patriotism, energy, and capital into the breach, sustained her credit, vindicated her good name, and won the gratitude and received the thanks of sovereign States. All this, fellow-citizens, is but the outlines of a portraiture and a grouping of some incidents in a sketch which I will not fill up, because recent events have spread before you the details and drawn the picture with colors of light."

The annexed obituary notice we have taken from a late number of the National Intelligencer, and which in itself will fully explain the object in having it herein inserted:

"Mr. ELISHA RIGGS, whose decease we announced yesterday, was one of the oldest and wealthiest bankers in the United States. He was born in Montgomery county, Maryland, in 1779, and first entered into business for himself at Georgetown, in the District of Columbia, where he resided for several years, during which period George Peabody, the wealthy London banker, then under age, was taken into partnership with him. They afterwards together established the house of Riggs, Peabody & Co., of Baltimore.

"In the course of time Mr. Riggs retired from that firm and removed to New York, where he resided for many years previous to his death, and where he always took an active part in all the leading enterprises of his time requiring large means and commercial experience. He was one of the most active friends of the New York and Liverpool line of steamships, and contributed largely towards its establishment. One of his sons is a partner with Mr. Collins in the agency of that line.

"Mr. Riggs died on the evening of the 3d instant, in the 75th year of his age, after an illness of several weeks. He was a man of strong domestic affections, and leaves a widow and six children, five of them sons, to mourn his loss. One of his sons, Elisha, is a member of the firm of Corcoran & Riggs, and his son George retired from the same firm a few years since with a large fortune."

With great pleasure our pen must here record the name of W. W. COR-CORAN, Esq., and that also of the late F. DODGE, Esq. A prominency of character belongs to these individuals, as connected with the annals

of our town, which the faithful chronicler must not overlook ; and for myself I have not the slightest disposition to be so recreant to our higher
nature as to forget their kind deeds and services. Our town is largely
indebted to them for many of its most valuable improvements and adorn-
ments ; its highest interests have been subserved by their efforts, and its
prosperity greatly accelerated and heightened.

To the liberality of the former we are, as a town, in possession of what
is termed the " Corcoran Charity Fund," a donation of ten thousand dollars, the interest of which is applied annually to the purchase of fuel for
the poor and needy who may be exposed to the inclemencies of our winters. To his munificence on a larger scale, and more commensurate with
his ample means, we owe the beautiful city of the dead known as " Oak
Hill Cemetery," which crowns our heights—a cemetery whose loveliness
and attractiveness is unsurpassed, and which, by its hallowed associations,
contributes so largely to the pleasures of both citizens and strangers who
may visit its sacred precincts or tread its sequestered walks, though to
many this pleasure is mingled with a sadness, relieved by the light which
streams upon the tomb from the promise of the resurrection morn. We
must here not forget to mention the fact that also our public school has shared
in his generous donations. Much encouragement has been given to this
institution by his fostering care. It was his intention a few years back
to have established and endowed a high school for the instruction of the
advanced pupils of the Georgetown school in the higher branches of mathe-
matics, philosophy, and the languages ; but this praiseworthy design was
thwarted by some who did not understand fully his purpose. We hope
he will yet carry out this scheme, which will be so fruitful of happy consequence to our youth.

Georgetown was the birthplace of W. W. Corcoran, Esq., yet he has resided for a number of years in Washington, where he has conducted, as
is generally known, an extensive banking business, and from which he has
expressed his purpose to retire as soon as practicable, he having amassed
sufficient wealth ; we might say a princely fortune, his assessable property being larger than that of any other person in that city. May he long
live to enjoy his merited affluence and the increasing esteem of his fellow-
men !

The late Francis Dodge, Esq., though not a native of this place, yet
it was his permanent home by adoption. He was born in the town of
Hamilton, Essex county, Massachusetts, August 9, 1782, and was there
educated by the celebrated Dr. Mannassah Cutler. He came to Georgetown in 1798, and made this place his home by adoption. As a merchant
he was widely known and respected. Owing to his ability and the extent
of his business, he exercised a controlling influence over our commercial
transactions. By perseverance, careful gardianship over his own affairs,
and foresight, he became one of our wealthiest and most prominent citizens. For a long term of years he was the representative of his fellow-
townsmen in our Corporate Councils. Upon all matters of public interest connected with the welfare and prosperity of the town, his judgment,
sound and discriminating, was consulted, and seldom was his decision upon any question overruled. As the author of the " sinking fund" scheme
he is entitled to our grateful remembrance—a scheme which has in a few

years liquidated some ten or fifteen thousand dollars of our funded debt, and which, in its future operations, is expected to liquidate it entirely.

"The sinking fund is progressing with the most encouraging success, and, if properly sustained by the corporate power, as I am sure it will be, it will accomplish its great work of extinguishing our debt in less than twelve years, without withdrawing a dollar from the treasury, and without imposing the slightest burden upon the pockets of the people."—[*Mayor's Message, March* 7, 1851.

With a mind strongly prudential, and always acting with marked integrity, he had strong claims upon the confidence of those by whom he was surrounded. We need not say that these claims were liberally regarded and freely acknowledged. In the midst of his usefulness, he was called by an All-wise Providence to throw of the mortal coil, and enter upon that state of existence when the mortal assumes the immortal, and the all-glorious body of the blest. Upon his demise our corporate authorities were not remiss in their duty to this eminent citizen. The following is the communication of the Mayor to the assembled Boards of Common Council and Board of Aldermen :

MAYOR'S OFFICE, GEORGETOWN, OCT. 9, 1851.
GENTLEMEN: I have to perform the meloncholy duty of announcing to you the decease of FRANCIS DODGE, Esq.,
His long and honorable career as a sagacious merchant, his uniform identity with enterprises for the advancement of the public good, his considerate and unobtrusive acts of benevolence, his exemplary purity of private life, and valuable services in our Corporation Councils, with but few and temporary intermissions, for the last forty-five years, call for your marked recognition and profound respect.
You are therefore assembled to make suitable arrangements for attendance at his funeral, and to give a becoming expression of your appreciation of the deceased's eminent merits, and the serious loss which has been occasioned by this mournful event.
Very respectfully, your obedient servant,
H. ADDISON, Mayor.
Hon. Board of Aldermen and Board of Common Council.

The following resolutions, more fully showing the respect of the Corporation, were passed :

WHEREAS we have heard, with sensations of profound sorrow, that Divine Providence has been pleased to remove from our midst by death our esteemed neighbor and fellow-citizen, FRANCIS DODGE, Esq.: Therefore—
Be it resolved, &c., That the members of this Corporation will proceed in a body from the Council Chambers, to attend the funeral of Mr. Dodge, as a mark of respect for the memory of a citizen of eminent usefulness, whose public spirit, wise counsel, and earnest interest in the welfare of Georgetown will leave a permanent influence on the affairs of the town, and entitle him to the lasting respect of its citizens.
And be it further resolved, That we deeply sympathise with the family of the deceased in their bereavement, and that a copy of these resolutions be presented to them by the Mayor.
Approved, *October* 10, 1851.

There is another name we may mention here in connection, with great propriety. I allude to the late JOHN PICKRELL, Esq. He was also a successful merchant, and for a long time a member of our Corporation; his judgment and experience were often called into requisition, and favorably esteemed. Upon his departure by death from our midst he was favored justly with like testimonials of our Corporation to the purity of his character and his faithful labors in behalf of the prosperity of our town.

These men, we are proud to say, commenced life depending upon their own exertions; and, without adventitious aids, they succeeded in their respective vocations; by their ability, indefatigable industry, and prudent speculations, they achieved honorable names and large fortunes. When they started in life their prospects were not as propitious or flattering as many of whom we might make mention among our young merchants. Their advantages and facilities were not half so great; and we note this fact that they may endeavor to follow more closely in their footsteps, adopt and carry into practice the business maxims and precepts which gave them such success. If not disposed to study the character of those who are or have been prominent and successful in our own field of commercial and mercantile labor, we would recommend them to purchase and peruse carefully a work with the title of "Successful Merchant," from the pen of W. ARTHUR, A. M. In this work they will find much to instruct them, and withal they may be profited.

A brighter period has begun to dawn upon our affairs as a community; and our aim by this imperfect article has been to urge on those who possess wealth and ability to consummate or complete those enterprises which have been commenced so energetically, but are, as yet, in embryo.

" Lives of great men all remind us
We can make our lives sublime,
And, departing, leave behind us
Footprints in the sands of time;
Footprints, that perhaps another,
Sailing o'er life's solemn main,
A forlorn and shipwreck'd brother
Seeing, shall take heart again.
Let us, then, be up and doing,
With a heart for any fate,
Still achieving, still pursuing,
Learn to labor and to wait."